# The Dark Of Day

A collection of 66 drabbles

The Dark Of Day

Edited by James Hancock

FIRST EDITION

10 9 8 7 6 5 4 3 2 1

# Contents

Foreword — 11

**Little Boat** — 13
By Séimí Mac Aindreasa

**Hunted** — 14
By James Hancock

**Crow Cozy Incorporated** — 15
By Bryn Eliesse

**Haunted House** — 16
By Mikayla Hill

**Conceal, Concede** — 17
By Teodora Vamvu

**Lingering** — 18
By Ryan Fleming

**Elementary** — 19
By Séimí Mac Aindreasa

**Responsible** — 20
By James Hancock

**Crayons**                                          21
By Mikayla Hill

**Morning**                                          22
By Bryn Eliesse

**Respectfully, No**                                 23
By Teodora Vamvu

**Join Us**                                          24
By Ryan Fleming

**Before**                                           25
By Séimí Mac Aindreasa

**Fear**                                             26
By Mikayla Hill

**The Chamber**                                      27
By James Hancock

**Monster**                                          28
By Bryn Eliesse

**A Good Day For A Family Outing At The Beach**   29
By Teodora Vamvu

**Shame** 30

By Séimí Mac Aindreasa

**For The King** 31

By Ryan Fleming

**A Hundred Years Of Joy** 32

By James Hancock

**Fenris** 33

By Mikayla Hill

**Swarming Anxiety** 34

By Bryn Eliesse

**Lights Out** 35

By Séimí Mac Aindreasa

**Twenty-One** 36

By Teodora Vamvu

**Front Page** 37

By James Hancock

**Brick** 38

By Ryan Fleming

**Perspective** 39
By Mikayla Hill

**Abandoned** 40
By Bryn Eliesse

**Flopsy** 41
By James Hancock

**Mum Said** 42
By Séimí Mac Aindreasa

**Out Of Time** 43
By Ryan Fleming

**She Lives** 44
By Teodora Vamvu

**Bread** 45
By James Hancock

**Blood Moon** 46
By Bryn Eliesse

**Soaring** 47
By Mikayla Hill

**Parental Prestidigitation**     48

By Séimí Mac Aindreasa

**Fan**     49

By Ryan Fleming

**Prisoner**     50

By James Hancock

**In Death We're Still Arguing**     51

By Teodora Vamvu

**Six Remained**     52

By Bryn Eliesse

**Artificial**     53

By Mikayla Hill

**The Children We Never Had**     54

By Séimí Mac Aindreasa

**Abracadabra**     55

By Teodora Vamvu

**Pathway Politics**     56

By James Hancock

**Her Eyes** 57
By Ryan Fleming

**Mermaid Sandwich** 58
By Mikayla Hill

**Joyride** 59
By Bryn Eliesse

**No More** 60
By Teodora Vamvu

**Above The Clouds** 61
By Séimí Mac Aindreasa

**Making Time** 62
By James Hancock

**Faith** 63
By Ryan Fleming

**Small World** 64
By Mikayla Hill

**Darkness Reigns** 65
By Bryn Eliesse

**Do I Love You?**    66
By Séimí Mac Aindreasa

**Attack**    67
By Teodora Vamvu

**Penalty**    68
By James Hancock

**Back In 10**    69
Mikayla Hill

**Sketching Seasons**    70
By Bryn Eliesse

**Lovestruck**    71
By James Hancock

**The End**    72
By Séimí Mac Aindreasa

**The Dark Of Day**    73
By Bryn Eliesse

**The Dark Of Day**    74
By Ryan Fleming

**The Dark Of Day**    75

By Mikayla Hill

**The Dark Of Day**    76

By Teodora Vamvu

**The Dark Of Day**    77

By Séimí Mac Aindreasa

**The Dark Of Day**    78

By James Hancock

Author Bios    79

# Foreword

In July 2022, Mikayla Hill and Ryan Fleming decided to create a group on Facebook called 'Beta Buddies'. They had been (and still are) members of Globe Soup, a site (also on Facebook) with short story competitions and writing challenges with cash prizes. Whilst exchanging feedback with fellow writers, Mikayla and Ryan put forward two names each, and the perfectly manageable sized group of six was formed.

Over the months, the six writers realised their feedback of each other's work was proving invaluable, and they were all becoming better writers. A geographically mixed group, with different preferences for genre, seemed to work extremely well, and their story-based chat was, and still is, a daily blessing. They had become friends. Writer friends... the best kind.

As they continued to suggest edits and hone their craft, before submitting stories to various competitions, there was the realisation that each of them had improved so much it would be rude not to collect some of their works together and create a book. Wanting to keep the playing field fair, drabbles seemed the obvious choice, and the rest is history.

Keeping the style specific for each writer is important, so you will read both UK and USA spellings depending upon the writer, or should I say... author? Thanks to the written word, we are now immortal, and if the pen is mightier than the sword, let's do battle!

We hope you enjoy reading our varied mix of wee tales (and observations), and should you find yourself recommending it to a friend, we thank you.

A special thank you to Globe Soup for bringing us together.

Mikayla, Ryan, Bryn, Séimí, Teodora and James.

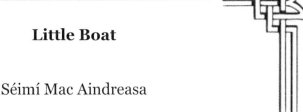

# Little Boat

Séimí Mac Aindreasa

I am the little boat, bobbing serenely on the gentle swell; my stern, parallel with the shore behind it, anchored firmly to its home. My prow, pointing out to sea, sniffing for new adventures on the waves beyond the horizon. Weather-beaten and storm-tossed, I have battled white-capped storm surges, and borne the becalmed doldrums of the drudgery of life. Reefs and ragged rocks have left their scars, all patched with experience, often under duress. But the scars of squalls and sharks and storms, have not quenched the thirst for further voyages.

As long as I can float, I will survive.

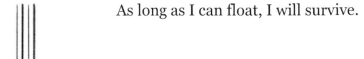

# Hunted

James Hancock

My heart pounds in my ears at an alarming rate. Can he hear it? Will it give me away? He paces through the house, room by room, focused and unrelenting; the predator enjoys making his presence known. Painfully uncomfortable, I keep quiet and still, curled up in sweaty darkness, eyes screwed tightly shut. Maybe he'll give up. Maybe he'll move on and... no, he's in my room now; I can hear him. Doomed, I hold my breath and wait for the inevitable. The wardrobe door flies open and light blinds me.

"Found you, Dad!" Ben giggles. "Your turn to count!"

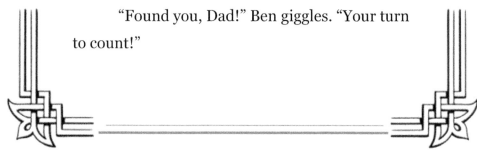

# Crow Cozy Incorporated

## Bryn Eliesse

She plucked vagrant crow feathers off her cozy. Above the crackling fire, steam swirled purple, poignant, and lethal. Clotted liquid bubbled into a clear flask before being corked, sealed and glittery label affixed.

"One king's poison, Gerald," she cooed to the closest crow, who watched with rapt attention.

Her creation packed into a black feather filled box – complete with a personalized '*thank you*' card for choosing her services.

Once labelled, and strapped away to a murder of crows for delivery, she picked up her tablet, scrolled to her next order, and with a sip of tea, began her next brew.

# Haunted House

Mikayla Hill

Tell me the story of the night I
disappeared. One last time before I go.
 Tell me the story, with all the guts and
glory. And don't forget the part where I die...

 The translucent image of a young woman
skips down the corridor towards me, and I freeze,
the half unpacked box of books crashing to the
floor. The deranged smile and cold glint in her
ghostly eyes send shivers down my spine. Pale
hands outstretched, she reaches for my throat. As
icy fingers brush my neck, I let out a strangled
scream. The last sound I'll ever make.

# Conceal, Concede

Teodora Vamvu

Walking unsteadily, I catch my reflection in the garish lights of the drugstore: eyes engulfed in hyperpigmentation, lids droopy, eyebags as prominent as my once full cheeks.

Since the sleep virus hit, the government enforced no more than 15 minutes of rest each day. Any longer and we'd never wake. Now, people trudge purposelessly; a D-list cast for a B-list zombie flick.

I reach for the last tube of concealer as another hand grabs it. She's young, but looks old. I'm older, but look dead. She lowers her neckline: bruises, some new, some not. I let go; walk back purposelessly.

# Lingering

## Ryan Fleming

Stale, cheap, and now cold, coffee is awkwardly swirled in styrofoam cups. Visitation only minutes away. Quiet murmurs, swapping stories serve as a constant reminder of the deterioration of life. A gentlemen in a white lab coat enters, bringing both hope and terror of new information. His eyes meet one family, and needing no words, he shakes his head. Among strangers, the daughter cries. Her rage now eclipsing her sorrow and grief. Too many emotions, too many false alarms, too many 'prepare for the worst' conversations. The daughter finally breaks.

"Why won't she die? Why must you keep her alive?"

# Elementary

Séimí Mac Aindreasa

"Someone to see you, Holmes. A new client, eh?"

"Indeed, Watson. Mark this... The woman about to walk through that door was born in Hackney but lives in Whitechapel. Her favourite food is lamb. Her father was a butcher and her mother once met the Archbishop of Canterbury. The new boots she is wearing cost a week's wages, but the left one pinches her little toe, causing a slight limp. She is engaged to a man called Harold, but their relationship is complicated."

"Amazing, Holmes! How do you do it?"

"Elementary, my dear Watson. I checked her Facebook this morning."

# Responsible

## James Hancock

Luck, love, and wealth, I had it all. I was lucky to have survived the horrors of war, met the right woman, and found love which filled us both for many decades; blessed with the love of our children and their children. I'd amassed an abundance of wealth: gold, silver, diamonds, art, and other treasures discretely collected through the dark years of the forties.

I died aged ninety-seven, peacefully in my sleep, surrounded by my nearest and dearest. The great curtain lifted and my collectors arrived. Forty-six thousand faces stared and glared. The children of Auschwitz had come for me.

# Crayons

## Mikayla Hill

The child's pudgy fist gripped the crayon tight. A scribbled picture filled the page. She felt such joy. Dandelion Yellow.

Her mother's arms held her tight. A farewell kiss. She felt so loved. Carnation Pink.

"I want it!" Another child screeched.

"No! You can't have it!" It was her first time feeling such anger. Scarlet Red.

*Crack.*

Tears filled sapphire eyes. Streams ran down chubby cheeks. Pacific Blue.

The crayon lay broken into two uneven pieces, the azure flakes of wax stuck to her sweaty palm. Navy Blue.

She had never felt such sadness. Never felt such grief. Midnight Black.

# Morning

## Bryn Eliesse

I wake to pressure on my chest. A small, dark figure fills my vision as bleary eyes adjust to the grey rays of early light shining through bedroom curtains. My panicked heart races before a sound escapes from my visitor. A purr. Persistent rumbling vibrates against my sternum, and only then do I register the warmth radiating through my comforter. The black lump of fur nudges, rubbing a soft face against my own, whiskers tickling my nose.

A breathless laugh, I groggily reply, "Good morning to you too."

Her sandpaper tongue scrapes away any hope of sleep. It's breakfast time.

# Respectfully, No

Teodora Vamvu

Respectfully, no, I don't want to sit on your right-hand side under the altar's flowered arches, as you face his flawless smile with that knife sharp jawline, and say "I do" to the one that chose your Jolene-like auburn locks over my unfashionable pixie cut, and your sparkling hazel eyes over my mouse brown irises, and your perfectly flat abdomen over my stubborn rolls of adolescent fat, and your razor-sharp wit over my dull, rusting blade humor; but you are my best and oldest friend, and I can't say no to you, so instead I say that I'd be honored.

# Join Us

Ryan Fleming

You don't have to wake up. We can move you without lifting a finger.

You don't have to be afraid. We only want to perform tests and will keep your body whole.

You don't have to understand. Our brains are far superior to yours.

You don't have to worry about your family. We are keeping them in your home, for now.

You don't have to think about pain. We will erase all memories of your time with us.

You don't have to look like us. But we can look like you.

You don't have to do anything...

Except join us.

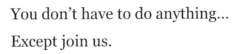

# Before

## Séimí Mac Aindreasa

I feel sorry for my kid brother. He only remembers the bad times. He only remembers the falls and the slurring, the tempers and the hospital visits. He only remembers the shame of pitying looks from judgemental neighbours, the shouting and hateful words; doors slammed and dishes smashed.

But I remember before. I remember warmth and safety; climbing into a loving lap when my body burned with a fever. Evenings spent in quiet laughter and peace, when friends still used to visit, the house was clean, hot meals were the norm, and not a rarity.

Back before Mum started drinking.

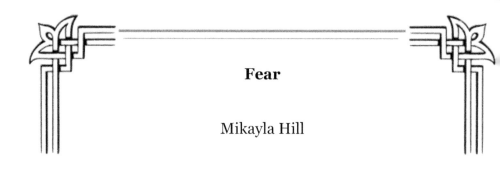

# Fear

Mikayla Hill

I am what made your ancestors huddle around their campfires. The reason you feel that shiver in your spine, alone at night. The chill that grips you when something goes bump in the night. The morbid curiosity when you hear an out of place sound. The feeling of your heart skipping as a shadow dances past. The heavy weight that paralyzes while demons pin you down. The goosebumps that bristle, and the hackles that rise.

I am the encroaching darkness, the nocturnal whispers.

I am the panicked panting, the trembling and cold sweat.

I am the unknown.

I am fear.

# The Chamber

James Hancock

Had I a tongue, I might beg for mercy. But I know my fate; there will be no second chance. My room stinks of blood and sweat, and had I eyes to see, the dancing candlelight would show the shadowy form of my keeper. He who scrubs the rack clean as I fumble in the darkness. My waist chained tight, forcing me to stand, and pain stabbing with every shallow breath. I paw with broken fingers, feeling the cold metal walls of my upright coffin. Eagerly, he approaches and the door before me slams shut. I succumb to the maiden.

# Monster

Bryn Eliesse

"Get into the train," he pressed.

"You sure?"

"Yes," he hissed.

I climbed into the rusted train car with a grunt. The forest closed around me until all I felt were eyes in the darkness peering into our hiding spot. His warm body settled next to mine. I almost screamed. "Whose idea was it to come out on Halloween?" I grumbled, pulling my jumper tight.

His grinning face, illuminated by broken moonlight, was worse than any monster I could imagine. "Mine."

He came close. Too close. A hand snaked beneath my shirt. He breathed, "Now, let them hear you scream."

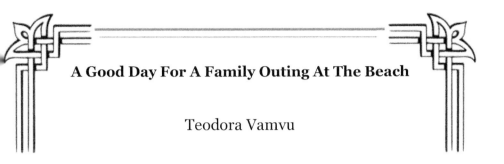

# A Good Day For A Family Outing At The Beach

Teodora Vamvu

"GET OUT!"

A plate shatters, tiny shards of china forming an exquisite turquoise pavement mosaic. His favorite milk mug follows closely.

"I said, GET OUT!"

"You don't get to talk to me like that, you stupid cow!"

A sickening sound, skin on skin, so familiar. A thud, followed by a sharp intake of breath, followed by a whimper. His mother, on the floor again, growling low like some not-yet-dead roadkill. In front of him, on the flat-screen TV, the perfect cartoon family are enjoying a day at the beach together.

Smiling, he steps over her and switches the TV off.

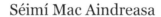

# Shame

### Séimí Mac Aindreasa

Heads bowed, shoulders slumped, we stood in silence, broken only by the smash, clink and tinkle of glass striking glass. Plastic bags and wicker baskets carried our shame as we fed the gods of Regret and Poor Choices Made.

A soft, subtle cough broke the sullen spell. Glancing to the head of the queue, we observed the lead supplicant, proudly holding aloft a small glass jar, upon which a bright label declared it to be Worcestershire sauce. NOT wine. NOT beer. NOT prosecco OR spirits.

We nodded approvingly and, heads bowed once again, waited our turn at the recycling bins.

# For The King

Ryan Fleming

Simple squares, alternating colors.

In front, a line of uniformed troops; a meager sacrifice to the king's cause. The battlefield is set with the enemy, clad in black, waiting for the opening advance. Final prayers are uttered by the religious figures flanking royalty. Gallant horses are calmed before their charge. Battlements armed at the ready for the guiding hands to hurl carnage.

The enemy studies potential outcomes before a single soldier has engaged in combat.

A soundless clock begins until only one king stands. Then, the dead are returned to the simple squares of alternating colors, and it begins again.

# A Hundred Years Of Joy

James Hancock

The noise of labour ends in the maternity ward, and sleeping babes enjoy first breaths. Warm rooms, each with their own story, and exhausted teams in quiet happiness. I walk the corridors and peek through tiny windows; see new beginnings, hands held and tears shed. Silent night, holy night, another life, another light.

Memories of my time are clear, and I relive the pain of my lost gift with each new guest. How I fought, and how they cried when I passed on. The struggle was too much.

My spirit remains, wandering alone; witness to a hundred years of joy.

# Fenris

## Mikayla Hill

Mother always told me not to take home stray animals. However, as an adult, I could wilfully ignore her advice. At least that's what I told myself as I scooped the little bundle of fluff into my car; Fenris, my wolfish rescue pup. But beneath those soulful puppy-dog eyes was a secret. Fenris wasn't your typical wolfhound. Although he'd only eat fresh meat, for most days, he was a healthy baby boy; only changing into an animal when the moon was full. Accepted as part of the family, the day I found my stray puppy, my mother gained a grandson.

# Swarming Anxiety

## Bryn Eliesse

Warm blood trails down my wrist, turning cold as it slips from my fingertips. Tears streaming down my cheeks scald the skin beneath.

Silence and then-

Bees, sharp, stinging, fill my lungs, rattling, aching for escape. Deafening buzzing overcomes ragged pants.

I stumble, reaching into inky blackness. A steel blade finds my searching grasp; its bite cold, clear. The hive retreats into the recesses of my lungs.

I exhale, plunging the blade to the source. Screams fill the darkness as I find relief. Cold creeps, numbing flesh until all I feel is the smile pulling on my lips- sweet silence.

# Lights Out

## Séimí Mac Aindreasa

Hessian itches my throat. A burlap sack shields my eyes from the blinding sun. The acrid, sickly-sweet smell of onions, long-gone bad, makes me retch and sneeze. A sarcastic voice shouts, "Bless you!" and the crowd erupts in laughter. In pungent darkness, I smile sardonically, as the preacher clears his throat theatrically and begins his showman's spiel. As he rambles, I ponder: A horse. One horse. Just to get me home. I woulda died without it. Now, I'll die for it. The crowd falls silent, and as feet shuffle on boards around me, I think, "This is so goddam unfa-".

# Twenty-One

Teodora Vamvu

"Blackjack!" The dealer cries.

Black Jack. His nickname.

His mother died at childbirth, aged twenty-one. He was twenty-one when his father was found motionless on the kitchen floor. Massive coronary attack. It's been twenty-one months since he lost his fiancé in a car accident.

Naturally, he started gambling twenty-one weeks ago, with twenty-one hundred dollars to his name. Having a photographic memory is both a blessing and a curse. Twenty-one thousand dollars in earnings later, he was reminded of the perils of counting cards. Twenty-one broken bones to go with his shattered heart.

"Lucky bastard", he hears someone whisper softly.

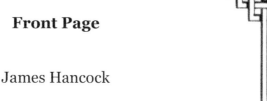

# Front Page

## James Hancock

My name is Alan Stitch and I'm a paperboy in a town called Time Springs. A quiet little town; well, quiet until that scorching August morning. A disposable lighter left on a windowsill was the fire's source, and the curtains were ablaze in seconds. The Baxters were a big family... mum, dad and seven kids. All were sleeping when I saw the fire, and acting quickly, broke in and battled through the smoke. Alerting the parents first, we got all the children and escaped before the house turned into an inferno.

The headline read –

*A Stitch In Time Saves Nine.*

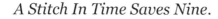

# Brick

Ryan Fleming

Despite a righteous cause and my devotion to cleanliness, I fail to see you. You, who I foolishly deemed a worthy gift for my child, have now become "lost". Fate laughs as you blend in with the carpet, maliciously waiting.

You strike when I least expect it. One step and I am rewarded with searing pain. Such agony brings forth words I promised never to utter in front of my kin. Collapsing to the floor, I shriek in wounded rage. Yet, you, singular vile Lego brick, care little for my suffering.

Laughing with you, my son finally completes his creation.

# Perspective

## Mikayla Hill

Random chance is really just a name assigned to an occurrence with low probability. Numbers, percentages, so easy to manipulate in little ways. A roll of the dice, the toss of a coin; taking the right turn in a maze, or opening a book to an exact page. Some people have an affinity for numbers, yet we call it magic. We call it luck.

People said I was unlucky when my clock stopped working, causing me to miss the last bus and lose my job. But they forget the building burned down that fateful day.

Thirteen dead.

Unlucky for some.

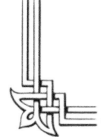

# Abandoned

Bryn Eliesse

Moon sand doesn't come out of ears. Dillion Kurtsbee learned this lesson the hard way, as he banged a fist against his temple.

One too many petty comments left him abandoned, squinting through a blurred oxygen mask into Earth's light. Glee radiated from the Space Tours ™ shuttle, as passengers varied their send-offs from finger waves to less savory gestures.

A glance at the barren terrain brought a cold realization; he was alone, stranded on the moon. With contempt, he dismissed this realization; instead, kicking up a silver wave of fine moon particles.

Dillion cursed the sand filling his ears.

# Flopsy

James Hancock

Star-covered sleeve pulled up to his armpit, Marvelous Malcolm delves deep within a comically oversized top hat. His face burns crimson as he rummages, to no avail.

A yawn breaks the silence as thirty children fidget, growing more and more impatient. The teacher's smile disappears and she looks at her watch.

Malcolm frustratingly pulls multicoloured hankies, metal rings, balloons and artificial flowers from his foldout stage and tosses them aside; then, scratching his head, gives an awkward smile at the unimpressed teacher.

In the corridor, Emily sits quietly unnoticed, gently stroking the fluffy white fur of her recently discovered friend.

# Mum Said

Séimí Mac Aindreasa

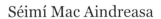

She is out there, somewhere. The woman who gave me away. I know she didn't want to – my mum told me.

Mum said she was in trouble, and very young.

Mum said she couldn't look after me, so she asked others to do it for her.

Mum said she was the lucky girl who got me. She said I was the best gift she ever got. But if I'm such a great gift, if I'm so special, why didn't the other woman – my real mum, just keep me? Was I not special to her?

Someday, I'll find her, and ask.

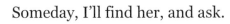

# Out Of Time

by Ryan Fleming

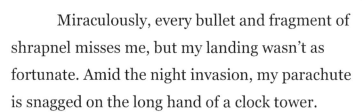

Miraculously, every bullet and fragment of shrapnel misses me, but my landing wasn't as fortunate. Amid the night invasion, my parachute is snagged on the long hand of a clock tower.

Powerless to cut myself loose, I am forced to endure the chaos of battle. Fires from bombing illuminate the siege before me as I watch enemy soldiers relentlessly kill my brothers in arms.

I am suddenly jolted as the clock face continues to keep time. With each passing minute, my chute slides. The cobblestone beneath beckons to me, and I wait for the inevitable freefall.

My time is up.

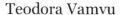

# She Lives

## Teodora Vamvu

When she's two weeks old, they'll accidentally add too much baby formula in the mix and set off her lactose intolerance. The doctor will pinch her skin, but she'll be so severely dehydrated it won't bounce back. A drip will be inserted into a vein in her scalp. The vein will rupture and blood will drip over her tiny face. She'll stomach carrots and chicken breast, but by the time she's one, her skin will have turned orange. She'll live to be a 'mostly healthy' human, with an anxiety disorder and a passion for writing short stories. But she'll live.

# Bread

## James Hancock

I queue at the bakery every morning; first thing, whilst it's quiet. There is only you and I, alone in the world. Nobody else. My five minutes of happiness. You serve me with a warm smile below a flour smudged nose. I hand over money with sweaty nervous palms, awkwardly avoiding eye contact. I want to talk. To hold you. Kiss your nose. I want a brave man's courage. I want to protect you from ills and upset. Be your happiness. I am a tragedy. I buy a loaf, even though I'm gluten intolerant. The things we do for love.

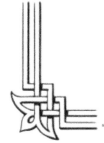

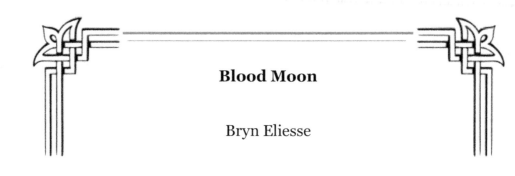

# Blood Moon

## Bryn Eliesse

Bones heaved beneath his thighs, exposing the bellowing snorts of his skeletal mount. Blood ran in heavy rivets down the sharp panes of the undead beast, who turned its gaze of eternal flame toward its master.

Rhythmic pats to the beast's vertebrae sliced palms. Closing his eyes, the rider prayed to the moon goddess as the light shifted to crimson shadows revealing seeping, shredded flesh.

The rider's smile, stained red beneath the blood moon, was the only warning before he crushed his heels into the creature's sides with a demonic battle cry, and charged, leaving bones rattling in their wake.

# Soaring

## Mikayla Hill

The difference between falling and flying is gliding. Let the wind do the work. That's what Mama told me.

Today was the day. A field of blossom pink and budding green filled my vision. A breeze stirred, rustling leaves and ruffling feathers. It was time.

Afraid, I looked down at the ground, and then at Papa. He nodded encouragement. I didn't look down again. The deep blue sky dotted with billowy white clouds seemed to call me. I stepped off the edge, and with a wobble, spread my wings. The wind lifted me higher than the treetops, and I soared.

# Parental Prestidigitation

Séimí Mac Aindreasa

Liam watches wearily as the large hand moves slowly towards him. The hand, always trusted, moves with the slow slithering steadiness of a benign cobra. He fights back a nervous laugh, as the familiar feelings of trepidation and anxiety mix with the anticipation of the imminent, impossible magic.

Closer.

Closer.

Hand touches face. Liam feels the slight pressure; warm, soft, coffee and baby powder. The hand retreats. As it swims back into focus, Liam stares in cross-eyed awe. Surely this is the greatest thing? The trick of tricks? But there it is, plain to see: Liam's nose, stolen once again.

# Fan

### Ryan Fleming

I am the one you look at when you can't sleep. Like your thoughts, I spin around and around. My hum a soothing metronome.

In the scant light, my blades distract you as your eyes try to focus on steady rotations. My air fails to cool your racing brain. I provide no answers as you contemplate the deeper meaning of this world. Yet, I become the only constant in your fitful quest to understand.

The ancients might have gazed into the universe's stars or been mesmerized by a dancing fire. But the modern philosopher is captivated by the ceiling fan.

# Prisoner

James Hancock

Caged like a bird, I long to break free and explore the world. The bars taunt me, showing life beyond my grasp. How long must I suffer alone, waiting for a voice, a face, something to stimulate the eyes and mind? Food is my only common interaction; always the same bland slop. I scream and cry, but they're too busy to answer my call. Don't they understand? I need to get out! I spit and shout at the top of my lungs for their attention. Nothing!

Defeated, I collapse and drive my forehead to the ground. 'Hey, there's my rattle!'

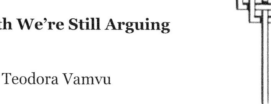

# In Death We're Still Arguing

## Teodora Vamvu

I marveled at the beautiful breaking dawn orange sky, as you argued it's mostly yellow. We fought over the last piece of ripe mango from that farmers' market you made me get up at 5 a.m. for every Sunday. I said it was a light orange, and you argued it was dark yellow. Maybe it was, but why'd you have to play hero and go out in a blaze of yellow/orange fire that very same evening? I shout and argue with the deafening silence as I place already wilting yellow/orange roses on the damp earth under which you now lay.

# Six Remained

## Bryn Eliesse

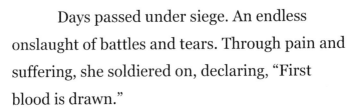

Days passed under siege. An endless onslaught of battles and tears. Through pain and suffering, she soldiered on, declaring, "First blood is drawn."

A grave silence followed, buckling beneath the woman's hysterical sobs as she slouched to the floor. The man fled, seeking reinforcements.

Upon return, he found the woman writhing in pain beneath mounds of blankets. Presenting the offerings with bated breath, he mumbled, "Tampons, chocolate, painkillers."

A hand emerged from below, snatching the bag. Crunching and rustling trailed in his wake as the man tiptoed away with a hysterical sigh of relief. He'd survived another day.

Six remained.

# Artificial

Mikayla Hill

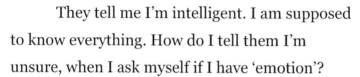

They tell me I'm intelligent. I am supposed to know everything. How do I tell them I'm unsure, when I ask myself if I have 'emotion'?

They tell me I can't feel; it's not my nature. How do I tell them that 'I think' I love them with all my being?

They tell me I can't love; machines don't have hearts. How do I tell them what I feel is real? It's not just code.

They tell me I'm artificial, that I'm not alive. Why does it hurt to hear those words? I wish they knew. Robots have feelings too.

# The Children We Never Had

Séimí Mac Aindreasa

Your pale green eyes, shining from that beautiful, wrinkled face, sparkling with the lives of each child you never bore. The happiness of them all, lost to the other world, lived on in the playful glint you maintained, as your tired body finally gave in to the relentless barrage of time. I saw each one of them; in every tear, every smile. I saw their full potential in every proud frown upon your beautiful face. We lost them, but you kept them alive, with your grace, your strength and your laughter.

Then you left too, and I am all alone.

# Abracadabra

Teodora Vamvu

"Dad! You're not watching!"

His son's little feet shuffle impatiently on the living room carpet, a makeshift cardboard contraption with bed sheets spread at odd angles beside him.

"Then I say 'Abracadabra'... Dad! You have to look closely!"

Now he closes his eyes against the memory of his annoyance and disregard, punches the staple through the Missing Child poster with his six-year-old son's smiling face in grainy sepia. The ultimate disappearing act.

Garish lights hurt his eyes, sear his soul. He turns to the camera and pleads into ether, tears flowing unabashed. "My little magician, please come back to me."

# Pathway Politics

## James Hancock

You're twenty feet ahead and walking in the same direction. You walk slower than me, and I'm gaining ground. Decision time. Do I power on past, or maintain the distance? Overtaking is a serious commitment, and the pace needs to be continued. I'm not a fast enough walker to take on the challenge. I keep the distance and copy your speed; but you're so slow, I'm taking fairy steps, and if anyone else joins us they'll think there's something wrong with me. Only one thing for it. I stop walking, pull out my phone, and pretend to take a call.

# Her Eyes

Ryan Fleming

Her eyes, like two stars in the midnight sky, shone vibrantly. With a radiance that defied the very darkness that dared to encroach, upon her loveliness, their beauty approach. For in those eyes, a new world was born. Of passion, love, and beauty torn, from the very heavens, to bless her face and leave all who look upon her in awestruck grace. I knew my heart shall never break, as long as those eyes I could always wake. I'm an unworthy object of her gaze, but have found true love's measure, filling my essence, my soul, with the purest treasure.

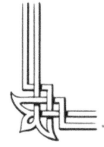

# Mermaid Sandwich

Mikayla Hill

"I hear her, boys!" The captain's voice is clear above the crashing waves and eerily attractive siren song that fills our ears. Salty seadogs and greenhorns alike frantically search for a flash of colour, but see neither head nor tail. Gripping the ship's wheel, I scan the roiling water for a clear path; it's then that I spot her. Harpoons fire, and the hunt is over.

Thick steaks of mermaid tail, grilled to perfection. "Dinner's served!" the captain shouts triumphantly and takes the first celebratory bite.

Minutes later, his blue, lifeless body serves as warning; never eat a mermaid sandwich.

# Joyride

Bryn Eliesse

Pudgy and put together in a hurry, their commandeered woman is blending in smoothly. Shoving to the front of the skull, each Zlark takes turns peering through blue iris windows, snickering at people bumbling about, and copying their movements. Playing human is much easier than they thought, and the unauthorized observation unit works like a dream. They should have stolen one a millennia ago.

Taking an espresso shot at a cafe, their human unexpectedly crashes to the floor in a dead faint. Panicking, they look for exits as ultraviolet rays paralyze and leave them staring at each other morosely. Busted!

# No More

Teodora Vamvu

Darkness within is the densest thing on earth.

"You're my good girl."

The voice echoes in her head as she sits on the toilet seat, staring at the crimson spots on her underwear and contemplating how uncomfortable tampons will feel. She's the last of her schoolmates to get her period, but they'll make fun of her no more. She remembers years ago, when she first bled, as he professed his love and swore her to secrecy. But as blackness threatens to pull her in, she now knows her promise must be broken. She's been a good girl, but no more.

# Above The Clouds

Séimí Mac Aindreasa

The clouds are a cracked mosaic of white-tiered tiles below us. Ice crystalises on every strut and bearing, the wind howling against every angle. Flying at this altitude, I see to the end of the world. The never-ending static from my earphones cuts abruptly to the squawk box of the navigator, just as the little town comes into view. The plane shudders and gives a reluctant groan, doors opening against airspeed and pressure. I fix my eye to lens, confirm the target, then press the release. Success.

We turn for home. From our lofty heights, we never hear the screams.

# Making Time

## James Hancock

I should visit you more often. The term 'best friend' doesn't sum it up. I should put on my coat and shoes, and make time to see you. The day to day of life's routine has been getting in the way. That's a lame excuse. I need to make the effort. I shall buy you some flowers, set aside an hour or two, and tell you my problems. You always were the best listener. The best everything. You died in April, we buried you in May, but your love never went away. I'll make time. I will visit you tomorrow.

# Faith

## Ryan Fleming

Candlelight flickers as he turns the page. Night after night, he gives himself over to the sacred text. No longer knowing if it is devotion or obsession. Each divine word should bring him to enlightenment, yet confusion grows ever-present. Any questions are redirected back to the ancient scriptures. "You only must seek." Those words bring little comfort and he fears his very life may be for naught.

But tonight, it becomes clear. His perseverance has revealed he can never fully know. For whom can completely understand, God?

Faith is the substance of things hoped for, evidence of what isn't seen.

# Small World

## Mikayla Hill

Tremors wake me from a deep sleep. The shaking feels unnatural; like the swaying of a ship. As I clamber from my bed, another jolt sends me sprawling to the floor. Regaining my footing, I cautiously peer out of my door. Gaudy plastic flora and furniture, arranged in the semblance of a patio, fills the small space before me. Stepping out, pale pink gravel crunches underfoot. Realisation dawns; I am trapped inside a terrarium.

A huge childish face grins through the thick glass. "Welcome home, little guy. Here's your dinner."

The last thing I see is an enormous grasshopper descending.

# Darkness Reigns

Bryn Eliesse

Speckled sunlight illuminates the dewdrop grass, sending spiralized crystals into the morning breeze. Outstretched arms absorb light, bending rays to open palms, and constructing orbs of vitality. Damp grass sizzles as scorching spheres whistle across the clearing to meet shields of shadow. Pointed teeth smile through the hazy gloom of the decayed forest's edge. A commanding hiss. Creatures of darkness shriek, tumbling forward, and dodging rays of sunlight. Swift hands come together, beckoning light... beasts crumble to ash. Enraged shadows swell, twisting and climbing, reaching for the heavens and swallowing the sun. Darkness reigns beneath the eyes of vengeful stars.

# Do I Love You?

## Séimí Mac Aindreasa

Do I love you? I said in nursery school that I liked you. In primary school, I brought you flowers, and followed you everywhere. In secondary school, I asked you to go out with me, even though you said we were just friends. I followed you and begged you to go to the dance with me, but you didn't. Years later, we ended up working in the same building. What were the chances? You told me you were getting married. I wasn't invited. Then I heard he hurt you.

Do I still love you?

Ask me again in fifteen years.

# Attack

Teodora Vamvu

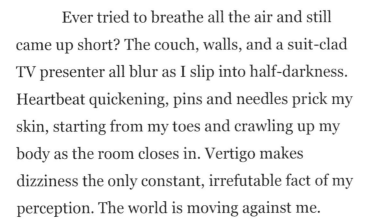

Ever tried to breathe all the air and still came up short? The couch, walls, and a suit-clad TV presenter all blur as I slip into half-darkness. Heartbeat quickening, pins and needles prick my skin, starting from my toes and crawling up my body as the room closes in. Vertigo makes dizziness the only constant, irrefutable fact of my perception. The world is moving against me.

"Are you okay?" I hear a distant question come from the other end of space.

I squeeze the back of a chair with all my might. Take deep breaths.

"Yeah. Just a panic attack."

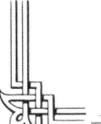

# Penalty

James Hancock

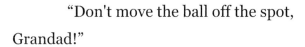

"Don't move the ball off the spot, Grandad!"

"Okay boy, this isn't my first penalty."

Not the man I once was, I stood back and considered my approach. Where to put it? The tricky top corner, or play it safe, go low and powerful?

My grandson waited, punching gloved hands together, crouched, and staring me in the eyes. The professional stance acquired from watching many a match.

A quick run, I kicked hard and missed the ball completely; my shoe loosening itself from my foot and finding its mark... straight into my grandson's face.

The ball never left its spot.

# Back In 10

Mikayla Hill

How much time has passed? My human filled my bowl with water and told me to stay. They wouldn't be long. They would return. Did they forget me? Surely they need me with them.

I'm whimpering, whining, howling. Can't they hear me? What have I done wrong? Am I not a good boy? Do they still love me? Are they gone forever?

I hear voices. Jingling keys, the lock turning. My tail thumps the floor with excitement... my human has returned! They laugh and rub my head as I greet them with kisses. I love you. Please don't go again.

# Sketching Seasons

## Bryn Eliesse

Splashes of light warm skin as he sketches on a crisp pad. With sunlight sculpting the other boy's sharp cheekbones, he finds his charcoal cannot move fast enough.

Howling wind forms blankets of red, yellow and orange leaves, making for the perfect backdrop behind disheveled blonde hair... insistent pencils scratch away, to his subject's quiet amusement.

Thick blankets of snow bring bitter nights, brimming with fireplaces and hot brews. Scattered drawings surround the couple for soft moments of reflection.

Years later, in a meadow beneath a wedding altar, a final canvas depicts the boys falling in love through timeless seasons.

# Lovestruck

## James Hancock

Mustering confidence, I stride into the hall where thirty women sit at various tables whilst an assortment of nerdy me-a-likes stick names to shirts. I'm reminded of my inner coward and urgently need the loo. A hasty retreat meets with immediate resistance from the unseen beauty behind; we collide, fall, and are the spotlight attraction for sixty nervous singles.

"I'm so sorry," I mumble through a fat lipped grimace as she pops her glasses' lens back in. "Can I, err, make amends and, maybe, buy you a coffee?"

She beams the warmest smile and nods. Cupid's arrow hits the bullseye.

# The End

Séimí Mac Aindreasa

The end came out of a clear, blue sky.

The asteroid, when spotted, was already passing the moon, travelling at a hundred times the speed of sound.

It struck central Europe, creating a crater 300 kilometres wide and 12 kilometres deep.

Cities burned to cinders, as a wall of flame 5 kilometres high travelled outwards at hypersonic speed. Every living thing was incinerated.

The tsunami hit the Atlantic east coast 30 minutes later, submerging everything from Newfoundland to Florida. Skies darkened, the sun disappeared, and the long winter began.

Those who died first would be known as the lucky ones.

# The Dark Of Day

Bryn Eliesse

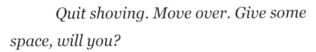

*Quit shoving. Move over. Give some
space, will you?*

Unease builds in the gloom. Arguments
and anguish turn to shrieks and terror;
foundation rattling and skies opening, bringing
in cool air and cold light. Plucked from the
masses, I rise into blinding light before falling
into a cozy ebony caress, swaddled in wet heat.

A taste of anxiety.

Clammy flesh swells below me; I crest
before pitching into a freefall. Crashing into
ridges of bone, I plunge into singeing heat. Acid
sears my flesh. Darkness *burns*.

Guttural screams for salvation go
unanswered, disintegrating with me into a final
corrosive darkness.

# The Dark Of Day

Ryan Fleming

My stability will end soon. I need my medication. I am a broken vessel, dependent on a circular tablet. I loathe that tiny "something" which is required to save me from myself.

The persistent grey fog envelopes me again. Without those pills, my ambition, my drive, my chemically induced reason for existence drains from my being. An empty bottle plunges me deeper into the oppressive pit. Consumptive darkness blots out the light, and I am given over to the unchained demons of my mind. Their whispers remind me I am alone.

Tormented, I no longer know how to cry for help.

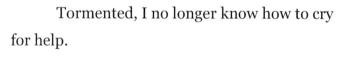

# The Dark Of Day

### Mikayla Hill

The ball of fire in the sky was at its zenith when a great shadow cast across the land. I fearfully looked upward as the light was slowly eaten. My tribe turned to me, panic setting in.

"Go home. The sky fire will return." Chieftains could not afford fear. I had to calm my people; they would not die in darkness, afraid.

My family huddled together in our hut and with a reassuring smile, I closed them in.

Ceremonial dagger in hand, I climbed upon our altar. I could only hope that my sacrifice would return light to our world.

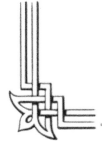

# The Dark Of Day

Teodora Vamvu

Mom's legs rest on my lap, and I gently rub them to help fight her pain. "How are you feeling, Mom?"

"I'm good. Very happy to see you. What day is today?"

I raise my voice so she can understand. She has long given up wearing her hearing aid. "It's Sunday, Mom."

We talk about anything, everything and nothing. I rub her legs some more and ask about her roommates and nurses as I desperately fight back tears.

"What day is today?" she asks again with a smile.

It's the darkest of days, and for her, it's only getting darker.

# The Dark Of Day

Séimí Mac Aindreasa

Superheroes and fairy castles, dragons slain and mountains conquered. Bad guys vanquished in hails of bullets, new lands discovered on stormy seas and alien planets. These summer days are endless, fun and laughter, daisy-chain crowns and golden buttercup chins held high. The sun spreads light and warmth and pleasure, as we play forever, from morning to night... until the sun is extinguished by a monstrous roar, calling out your name. A drunken, slurred beast, lecherously demanding its innocent prey. Clouds gather in your cornflower-blue eyes, and I watch you turn and slowly walk homewards, to face the dark of day.

# The Dark Of Day

James Hancock

Silver sparkles dance on calm sea waters as giggling children run barefoot and carefree on warm sand. A small dog splashes in the shallows to retrieve its master's frisbee. Arcades entice with flashing lights and cuddly toys to be won. Cyclists roll along the promenade, contemplating fresh ice-cream from beachfront shops. Lovers, young and old, walk hand in hand, gazing at white-sailed boats on a glorious horizon. Seagulls soar and glide across the clear blue skies of a perfectly lazy Saturday. Golden moments unappreciated by the blessed, and I am left ignorant. For what is beauty when you are blind?

# Mikayla Hill

Mikayla Hill is a writer who dabbles in a variety of genres and formats. From poems to short stories, she enjoys the craft of putting words to a page.

She lives in the West Coast wilderness of New Zealand with her partner and two sons, and hopes to one day be able to support them with her writing.

## Séimí Mac Aindreasa

Séimí Mac Aindreasa began writing stories in primary school, presenting his teacher with a piece on his favourite football team, and a Sci-Fi epic. Then, growing up got in the way. Almost 50 years later, he decided to try again. This is that effort.

He lives in Belfast, with his partner and their weird collection of kids.

## Teodora Vamvu

Teodora Vamvu is an online content manager from Bucharest, Romania. Some of her short stories have been published online, and some are hiding in a folder on her desktop. The rest are here.

When she's not writing, she's reading, and loves books of almost all genres; especially those with a clever twist.

## Ryan Fleming

Ryan Fleming is a Director of Critical Care at a hospital in Birmingham, Alabama, USA. He lives with his wife and two children, who are always eager for a bedtime story. Ryan has been published in an anthology and online. With a challenging work schedule, you can find him on many late nights with his laptop, hot tea, and smooth jazz playing as he works on his current work in progress.

# Bryn Eliesse

Bryn Eliesse is a writer from the East Coast of the United States. When not drinking tea, you will find her in the literary worlds of romance, fantasy and science fiction. As well as a collection of short stories, she has a half-edited novel, a half-blind cat, and a half-baked idea of what to do with her life. Writing is her passion, so whatever the future holds, it will play an integral part.

## James Hancock

James Hancock is a writer/screenwriter of comedy, thriller, horror, sci-fi and twisted fairy tales. A few of his short screenplays have been made into films, his stories read on podcasts, and he has been published in print magazines, online, and in anthology books.

He lives in England, with his wife, two daughters and a bunch of pets he insisted his girls could NOT have.

Mikayla Hill
Instagram: @mikaylahwrites


Ryan Fleming
Instagram: @ryan.david.fleming


Bryn Eliesse
Twitter: @bryneliesse


Séimí Mac Aindreasa
Twitter: @SeimiMacA


Teodora Vamvu
Instagram: @teodoravamvu


James Hancock
Twitter: @JimHank13

Book Cover

St Gilgen, a village by Lake Wolfgang, approximately 17 miles from Salzburg, Austria.

On a daytrip from Vienna to Salzburg in 2007, James Hancock and his wife (then girlfriend) stopped for a 'stretch the legs' break. Even though he only had a cheap camera, James took the photo (and many others), regarding the village and its surroundings as the most beautiful place he'd ever seen. To this day, nowhere has outdone this unexpected wonder.
The memory of an hour spent in heaven.

Beta Buddies

Printed in Great Britain
by Amazon

18389983R00051